Hand claps and finger snaps,
Hand claps and finger snaps,
Hand claps and finger snaps,
Hand claps…
And finger snaps.

Hand Claps, have some fun,
Finger Snaps, ev'ry one,
Music takes you anywhere,
'Cross the ground, through the air.

It takes you for a magic ride,
Up and down, side to side,
It's not as hard as it may seem,
All you have to do is dream…

THE GINGERBREAD MAN
as told by
Pieces of 8

Charles Mead, Story and Music
Steve Neale and Bill Schwartz, Illustrations

LIBRARY OF CONGRESS CATALOGING-IN-PUBLICATION DATA

Mead, Charles

The gingerbread man : as told by Pieces of 8. / Charles Mead
32 p. 11 x 8 1/2 $17.95
Includes illustrations, audio cassette
ISBN 0-918812-84-4

Book:
  Editor: Carl Simpson
  Typesetting and Prepress: A-R Editions, Inc., Madison, Wisconsin
  Printing: A-R Editions, Inc., Madision, Wisconsin

Educational Consultant: Jenifer Hartman

Audio Cassette:
  Producers: Ray Sherrock and Charles Mead
  Engineer: Tim Albert
  Recorded at Jacobs Ladder Productions, Saint Louis, Missouri
  Duplication: World Media Group, Inc., Indianapolis, Indiana

First Printing: March, 1995
PRINTED IN USA

THE GINGERBREAD MAN

as told by

Pieces of 8

Charles Mead, Story and Music
Steve Neale and Bill Schwartz, Illustrations

MMB
MMB MUSIC, INC.

This book is dedicated to Bill Reeder, who envisioned Pieces of 8.

Debby Lennon   Robin Woodrome
Annie Custer   Linda Walsh
Tom O'Brien   Ray Sherrock
Steve Milloy   Steve Neale

Charles Mead, Artistic Director
Charles Robin, Company Manager
Ayse Erenmemis, Director of Marketing
Tim Albert, Sound Engineer

For information on Pieces of 8

Drive All Night Productions
9666 Olive Boulevard, Suite 370
Saint Louis, MO 63132 USA
Phone: (314) 993-2432

A brief, meaningful and effective set of associated learning activities is available at no cost from

MMB Music, Inc.
Contemporary Arts Building
3526 Washington Avenue
Saint Louis, MO 63103-1019 USA
Phone: (314) 531-9635 or (800) 543-3771 (USA / Canada)
Fax: (314) 531-8384

Once upon a time...

There was a little old woman,
She lived together with a little old man,
They lived together in a little old house,
They had no children.

Then one day the woman said to herself,
"I can make us a child of our own,
I will make us a Gingerbread Boy,
He will live here in our home."

And with that, the woman went into the
kitchen and began to mix together
all of the ingredients that it takes to
make gingerbread cookies...

She mixed some flour
    and she mixed some sugar,
She mixed some salt
    and some molasses,
She mixed some butter and
    she mixed in some spices,
She would make their
    dreams come true.

"Oh, Gingerbread Boy,
    we'll love you,
Oh, Gingerbread Boy,
    yes you,
You will make our
    dreams come true."

When the woman had finished
mixing all of the ingredients
together, she took the dough
out of the bowl and laid it
on the kitchen table.

First, she carefully rolled out the dough.
Then, she took some scissors and
cut the dough into the shape of a
Gingerbread Boy.

She placed the Gingerbread Boy on a
cookie sheet, put the cookie sheet into the
oven, and sat down in a chair next to
the oven to wait.

The woman began to dream
about the Gingerbread Boy,
the little boy she and her
husband had always wanted.

Soon, she was fast asleep.

She would make him
a coat of chocolate,
It would have
cinnamon buttons,
He would have
a sugar-sparkle smile, and
two big gumdrops for eyes.

"Gingerbread Boy, we love you.
Oh, yes, we love you,
Gingerbread Boy,
Gingerbread Boy,
Gingerbread Boy,
We love you."

Suddenly, the oven door fell open
and the freshly–baked Gingerbread Boy
jumped down from the cookie sheet onto the
kitchen floor.
He saw the old woman sleeping in the chair
next to the oven.

He tiptoed quietly past her into the living room.
The old man was asleep on the sofa by the fireplace.
So the Gingerbread Boy walked to the door,
took one last look back, tossed his head in the air
with a laugh and ran from the house!

"No! No! No!
Oh, please don't go,
No! No! No!
Oh, please don't go,
No! No! No!
Oh, no! No!
No! No! No!
No! No! No!

"Gingerbread Boy,
Oh, please don't go!
No, Gingerbread Boy,
Don't go! No!!
Gingerbread Boy,
We love you so,
Oh, please don't…No!!

"Gingerbread Boy,
Oh, please don't go!
No, Gingerbread Boy,
Don't go! No!!
Gingerbread Boy,
We love you so,
Oh, please don't…No!
Don't go! Oh, no!!"

But the Gingerbread Boy
just looked back and said,

"I don't need you old woman,
I don't need you old man,
I don't want to live in your dark old house,
You'll never catch me...

"I'm the Gingerbread Man.
No, you never can,
No, you never can."

So the Gingerbread Boy he walked on
'til he came to a field...

...and in that field was a cow, and the cow said,

"Gingerbread Boy, come over here,
I'd like to eat you for lunch!"

*But the Gingerbread Boy
just laughed and said,*

"I ran away from the old woman,
I ran away from the old man,
I ran away from the old house in the country,
And I can run away from you Mrs. Cow—
Right now!

"You c-c-can't catch me,
I'm the Gingerbread Man,
You c-c-cannot catch me,
Run as fast as you can.
You c-c-can't catch me,
I'm the Gingerbread Man,
You c-c-c-c-can't catch me,

"I'm the Gingerbread Man!
No, you never can!"

So the Gingerbread Boy he walked on
'til he came to a pasture...

...and in that pasture was a horse, and the horse said,

"Gingerbread Boy, come over here,
I'd like to eat you for lunch!"

But the Gingerbread Boy
just laughed and said,

"I ran away from the old woman,
I ran away from the old man,
I ran away from the old house in the country,
I ran away from the cow in the field,
And I can run away from you Mr. Horse—
Of course!

"You c-c-can't catch me,
I'm the Gingerbread Man,
You c-c-cannot catch me,
Run as fast as you can.
You c-c-can't catch me,
I'm the Gingerbread Man,
You c-c-c-c-can't catch me,

"I'm the Gingerbread Man!
No, you never can!"

So the Gingerbread Boy he walked on
'til he came to the woods...

...and in the woods was a bear, and the bear said,

"Gingerbread Boy, come over here,
I'd like to eat you for lunch!"

But the Gingerbread Boy
just laughed and said,

"I ran away from the old woman,
I ran away from the old man,
I ran away from the old house in the country,
I ran away from the cow in the field,
I ran away from the horse in the pasture,
And I can run away from you Mr. Bear—
I can run anywhere!

"You c-c-can't catch me,
I'm the Gingerbread Man,
You c-c-cannot catch me,
Run as fast as you can.
You c-c-can't catch me,
I'm the Gingerbread Man,
You c-c-c-c-can't catch me,

"I'm the Gingerbread Man!
No, you never can!"

The Gingerbread Boy walked on down the road,
The road ended at the river,

A fox sat waiting by the side of the river,
"Gingerbread Boy, I'll be your friend."

"Those other animals they all tried to hurt you,
But not me, I will always be your friend,
Come, hop up on my back, we'll swim 'cross the river,
There is magic on the other side."

The Gingerbread Boy liked the fox.
Life with him would be so much more fun
than life with the old man and the old woman.

So the Gingerbread Boy climbed up on the fox's back,
and the fox began to wade out into the rushing water.

Soon, the water got so deep that it began to come up
over the fox's back, right to the Gingerbread Boy's feet!

"Don't worry," said the fox.
"Climb up on my neck.
It's much safer there."
So the Gingerbread Boy
quickly scampered from the
fox's back up to his neck.

The water was moving very fast, but he wasn't afraid.
He knew his friend the fox would protect him. Just then,
the water got even deeper. It was up to the fox's neck!

"Quick," said the fox.
"Jump up on my nose.
It's the safest place of all."

So, the Gingerbread Boy
jumped up on to the fox's nose.
It was wonderful there!
He could see everything that
awaited him and the fox
on the other side.

Suddenly, just as the fox reached
the river bank and began to climb
out of the water...

...he threw back his head and into his mouth fell the Gingerbread Boy!!

"No! No! No!
Oh, please don't go,
No! No! No!
Oh, please don't go,
No! No! No!
Oh, no! No!
No! No! No!
No! No! No!"

Never walk away from the ones who love you,
Make the people who care a part of your plan,
No, never walk away from the ones who love you,
Or you could suddenly end up...

Never walk out, never walk out,
Never walk out, never walk out,
Never walk out, never walk out,
Or you could suddenly end up...

...like the Gingerbread Man!